Squirrels

Quinn M. Arnold

CREATIVE EDUCATION
CREATIVE PAPERBACKS

seedlings

Published by Creative Education and Creative Paperbacks
P.O. Box 227, Mankato, Minnesota 56002
Creative Education and Creative Paperbacks are imprints of
The Creative Company
www.thecreativecompany.us

Design by Ellen Huber; production by Dana Cheit
Art direction by Rita Marshall
Printed in the United States of America

Photographs by Alamy (Robert Eastman, Cheryl Fleishman, Panther Media GmbH), Dreamstime (Robert Wisdom), iStockphoto (Dgwildlife, Dovapi, GlobalP, hardeko, itsjustluck, jillyafah, Kenneth_Keifer, Mr_Twister, Nataba, pidjoe, Preto_perola, pshenina_m, Rickochet, SallyNewcomb, sergeyryzhov, SumikoPhoto, Terryfic3D), Shutterstock (Maksimilian)

Library of Congress Cataloging-in-Publication Data
Names: Arnold, Quinn M., author.
Title: Squirrels / Quinn M. Arnold.
Series: Seedlings: Backyard Animals.
Includes bibliographical references and index.
Summary: A kindergarten-level introduction to squirrels, covering their growth process, behaviors, the backyard habitats they call home, and such defining features as their bushy tails.
Identifiers: LCCN 2017051387 / ISBN 978-1-60818-976-2 (hardcover) / ISBN 978-1-62832-603-1 (pbk) / ISBN 978-1-64000-077-3 (eBook)

Subjects: LCSH: Squirrels—Juvenile literature.
Classification: LCC QL737.R68 A7627 2018 / DDC 599.36/2—dc23

CCSS: RI.K.1, 2, 3, 4, 5, 6, 7; RI.1.1, 2, 3, 4, 5, 6, 7; RF.K.1, 3; RF.1.1

First Edition HC 9 8 7 6 5 4 3 2 1
First Edition PBK 9 8 7 6 5 4 3 2 1

TABLE OF CONTENTS

Hello, squirrels!

Bushy-tailed squirrels are backyard animals.

Most live in trees.

Tree squirrels have strong arms and legs.

Sharp claws help them climb.

They run and jump from tree to tree.

Furry squirrels can be brown, red, gray, or black.

Many have lighter-colored bellies.

Squirrels store nuts for winter.

They eat berries and insects.

They steal seeds
and birds' eggs.

Squirrels build **dreys** or hide in trees.

Baby squirrel pups are born blind.

They have no fur at first.

A squirrel buries nuts.

It runs up a tree.

“Kuk-kuk-kuk!” It flicks its tail and chatters.

Goodbye, squirrels!

Picture a Squirrel

eye
claw
foot

Words to Know

dreys: large, enclosed nests made from twigs, set high in a tree

insects: animals that have three body parts and six legs but no bones

Read More

Borgert-Spaniol, Megan. *Baby Squirrels.* Minneapolis: Bellwether Media, 2016.

O'Brien, Lindsy J. *Squirrels.* Mankato, Minn.: Creative Education, 2017.

Websites

National Geographic Kids: Eastern Gray Squirrel
https://kids.nationalgeographic.com/animals/eastern-gray-squirrel/#eastern-gray-squirrel-tree.jpg
Read more about the common Eastern gray squirrel.

PBS Kids: Wild Kratts Go Nuts!
http://pbskids.org/wildkratts/games/go-nuts/
Help a squirrel gather nuts in this game.

Note: Every effort has been made to ensure that the websites listed above are suitable for children, that they have educational value, and that they contain no inappropriate material. However, because of the nature of the Internet, it is impossible to guarantee that these sites will remain active indefinitely or that their contents will not be altered.

Index